For Rafael, with love, Aunt Fiz – EA

For Fiz, Kayt and Strawberrie, for your amazing support
and for always being fabulous to work with – KH

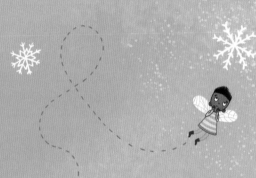

First published in 2019 by Scholastic Children's Books
Euston House, 24 Eversholt Street
London NW1 1DB
a division of Scholastic Ltd
www.scholastic.co.uk
London – New York – Toronto – Sydney – Auckland
Mexico City – New Delhi – Hong Kong

Text copyright © Emma Adams 2019
Illustrations copyright © Katy Halford 2019

PB ISBN 978 1407 19778 4
C&F PB 9781407198828

1 3 5 7 9 10 8 6 4 2

The moral rights of Emma Adams and Katy Halford have been asserted.

FSC
www.fsc.org
MIX
Paper from
responsible sources
FSC® C023419

Emma Adams and Katy Halford

Unicorn
and the
Rainbow Snow

SCHOLASTIC

There's a land far away
where the sky is so blue,

and anything can happen
– your **dreams** can come true.

It is **always** summer and wonderfully warm,
there's **never** a dark cloud and **never** a storm.

From when the sun rises until the day's done,
it's a place filled with **magic, wonder** and **fun.**

Early one morning, on the town's cobbled street,
as **dragons** flew by and small birds sang, **tweet, tweet,**
the people of Happyville skipped here and there
and ran all their errands with typical flair.

There's dear Unicorn,
with her bright **rainbow** mane,

and – look! –

there's a **knight**
singing love songs (again).

Can you see the **elves**?
Oh they're baking a cake,

while **Witch** eats an ice cream
(the one with the flake).

But . . .

"Oh gosh," said Rapunzel,
now starting to stare,
"Just **what** is that **thing**
in the sky over there?"

"A storm cloud!" said Witch,
"But **why** is it here?

We don't want grey clouds –
all we want is good cheer."

They watched it get closer and closer until,
Huddling together they felt quite a chill.

"It's cold!" said the wizard.
"But how can this be?"

WEATHER SPELLS
ALL YOU NEED TO KNOW

'It's never been cold here!"
cried the elves (there were three).

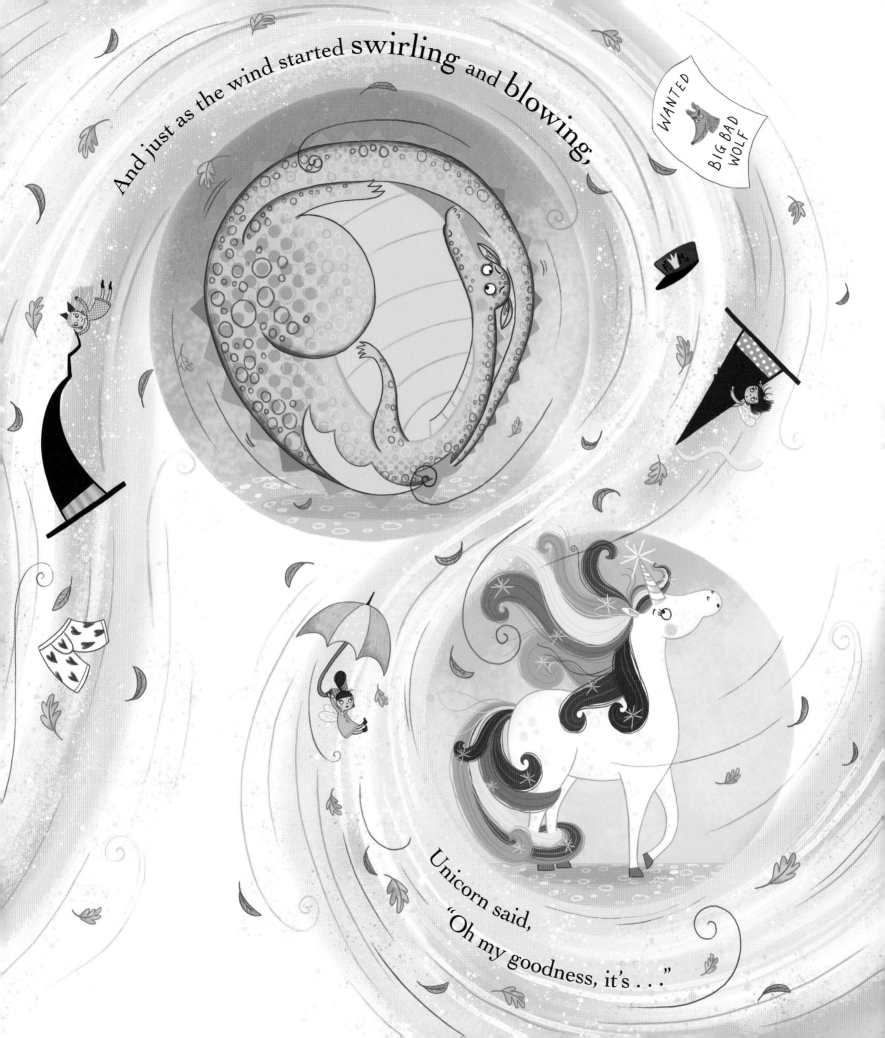

And just as the wind started swirling and blowing,

WANTED
BIG BAD
WOLF

Unicorn said,
"Oh my goodness, it's . . ."

"...snowing!"

She was right! Tiny snowflakes, each perfectly rare,

shimmered and shone as they danced through the air.

"Don't be afraid," she said,
"You mustn't run,
because here is a secret:
snow is . . ."

"...really fun!"

She led them through brilliant, **sparkling** white,
as snow fell upon almost all things in sight.

She had an idea (it's a great one, I'd say),
because, there in her stable was a ...

BIG SLOPE

TOWN

UNICORN'S STABLE

. . . beautiful sleigh.

The next thing you know,
the whole town was abuzz . . .

Who wants a sleigh ride?

Oh, everyone does!

They whizzed through the town and they zoomed through the street.

"Yippee!" cried out Knight, "this sleigh ride is a **treat!**"

They came to a stop with a small, icy skid.

And for the rest of the day,
can you guess what they did?

The elves went **ice skating** on their **outdoor pool.**

And Princess built **igloos** – **wow,** that looks so cool!

The fairies made **snow cones**,
full up to the brim,

while Wizard made **sculptures**
that looked just like him.

The witches went **sledging**,

then built things
with snow,

and everyone skied

(although Unicorn was slow).

HELP!

Then as it got dark and the day turned to night,
the fireflies appeared with their **beautiful** light.

Sleepy and happy,
they returned to their homes.

Big SLOPE

TOWN

SNOWDROP
CORNER

All of them smiling –
yes, even the gnomes.

Then . . .

as they **snuggled**
in bed,

and closed their tired eyes,

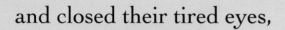

Unicorn busily planned
a **surprise.**

As everyone slept, as they snored, turned and tossed,
Unicorn walked through the icy, white frost.

She was very excited, and let out a
"Whoop!"

She had a big plan, all she needed was . . .

. . . POOP.

The very next morning, Happy Town was aglow,
with the most **beautiful, magical** . . .

... rainbow snow!

There's a land far away where the sky is so blue,
and anything can happen –
your dreams can come true.

WE ♥ UNICORN

YAY FOR UNICORN

It's not always summer – winter winds also blow,
so **three cheers** for Unicorn
and her **rainbow snow!**